c

o

p

e

Cover by *Alban Fischer*
CCM Design by *Michael J Seidlinger*
ISBN - 978-1-937865-41-2

For more information, find CCM at:

http://copingmechanisms.net

KATIE JEAN SHINKLE'S

THE ARSON PEOPLE

For Jay @ 6821 S. Forest Street

Acknowledgments

Thank you to The Butter/The Toast and The Collagist where excerpts have previously appeared. Thank you to Michael J. Seidlinger & Civil Coping Mechanisms, Jay Sorensen, Andrew Wickliffe, and Mom/Joe.

Pages 3, 5, 9, 15, 18, 36 borrow language from the penal codes regarding arson and burning from the states of Michigan, Illinois, Ohio, and Indiana.

For more content, find *The Arson People* on Vimeo:
https://vimeo.com/channels/thearsonpeople

STATE PENAL CODE (Excerpt)
Chapter XX
Arson & Burning

Section X00.110   Definitions

Sec. 110.

Any individual found engaging in the following definitions as it pertains to and is defined by the law could be found guilty of committing First, Second, Third, Fourth, or Fifth Degree Arson.

Unless the context requires otherwise, the following terms have the following meanings:

(a) "Burn" means setting fire to, or doing any act that results in, the starting of a fire, or aiding, counseling, inducing, persuading, or procuring another to engage in such action.

997 Jug Factory Road

In the middle of the night this hot summer night Elsie Davis sneaks out of her 2nd story bedroom window, slides herself down the front of the roof, drops herself onto the porch, and sprints through the woods separating her grandmother's house and two streets over. Before she enters the woods, she grabs a full, red, generic metal gas can and a box of GoGreen! kitchen matches she hid underneath the formica trestle attached to the front of the house. She called the elderly neighbor to the west earlier in the day when she knew her grandmother was out of gasoline to see if he had any. She always puffed her chest up extra when she had to make those phone calls, wanted to try to get in touch with a deeper voice inside, the man she knew she was. Even in summer she wears the heaviest clothing, today is a red and black plaid long-sleeved shirt with the sleeves rolled up and black leggings too small for her, which roll down. The neighbor called back but her grandmother answered, no gas for her. Later, Elsie Davis ate, sat on the corner of her bed until dark, and now she and the gasoline are leaving, around the half-fence her grandparents built to keep the raccoons out of the garbage. She is going as fast as she can through the woods. She is going to set Amber's house on fire. She is going to burn that bitch up.

STATE PENAL CODE (Excerpt)
Chapter XX
Arson & Burning

Section X00.110   Definitions

Sec. 110.
Unless the context requires otherwise,
the following terms have the following
meanings:

(b) "Individual" means any and all in-
dividuals and parties involved up to
and including those "burned" and those
that engage in acts of arson and burning, see (X00.100, Sec. 110, (a)).

112 Sprawl Road

Octavia is driving the car, Elsie Davis's grandmother's Cadillac, which they stole. They are keeping the headlights off but it is making it hard to see so every once in a while Octavia flashes the low beams. "We made a wrong turn. Let's go back," Octavia says and she puts it in reverse, mud and no traction. "We're going to have to rock it out," she says. Brewer and Elsie Davis get out and push the back end as Octavia, with the driver's side door open, guns the engine.

"One, two, three," Brewer grunts deeply, the car finally gives way, Elsie Davis falls knee first into the mud. Octavia barrels the car through the woods, leaving Brewer and Elsie Davis to walk the rest of the way to the house.

An extremely small, rustic cabin in the middle of nowhere is where Amber lives with her pedophile mother and mentally disabled older sister. Amber wears roller skates all the time and destroyed Elsie Davis's mini-trampoline once while jumping on it, popped a hole right through the top with one of the back wheels. Setting this particular house on fire feels hard for Elsie Davis. The place is so small: two windows, front and back, no stories, no front or back porch, a tiny concrete platform outside the sliding glass door (which doubled as the second window) and one vinyl braided beach chair, dirty, faded from the sun.

Elsie Davis knew the rumors about Amber's mother. Cut

to the past: a young woman of only eighteen ran the only child care facility in town out of her house and got caught touching the older boys (eleven, twelve, thirteen respectively), how she got caught Elsie Davis did not know, and, years later, it all came to light. Amber's mother was shut down, and instead of fully relocating came out here with her two children. This cabin is all she has. This cabin with a sign outside every Halloween that says no child can ring for candy.

Amber's mother was currently screaming at her daughter, calling her a worthless fat piece of shit. When Elsie Davis hears this, it, for one brief moment, makes her feel sad for Amber, sorry for her.

8 Monte Vista, #9

Octavia and Brewer's mom is and was never around and
so Octavia was home alone in an apartment a lot with
her little brother, no more than a few years their junior,
and Elsie Davis and Octavia and Brewer all hung out
there all the time, today being no different than any other
day.

Elsie Davis and Octavia and Brewer are together when
they first hear about Gretchen. Girl Found Dead in Lake
Michiganà Girl Found Dead in Lake Michigan Has Yet
to Be Identified Due to the Violent Nature of the Assault à Girl Found Dead Has Been Identified as 17 Year
Old Gretchen Steinberg. A week later: Girl Found Dead,
17 Year Old Gretchen Steinberg, Autopsy Reports Show
Sexual Assault.

They are glued to the TV the entire day, cancelled their
other plans with other people. They fielded phone calls
but had no answers. They knew, however, who commit-
ted this crime. They knew before the boys were arrested,
arraigned, got off. The media sympathized with them
and their "blemish" in their decision-making; even this
girl, Amber, who filmed it on her phone and did nothing
to stop it, even when the footage shows Gretchen pleading with her, begging her to intervene, even this girl got
sympathy for crying in court.

Gretchen Steinberg is raped by young men from their
high school and then beaten to death and left in Lake

Michigan and the young men walk. Here is where Elsie Davis and Octavia and Brewer decide to start paying
visits.

STATE PENAL CODE (Excerpt)
Chapter XX
Arson & Burning

Section X00.110   Definitions

Sec. 110.
Unless the context requires otherwise, the following terms have the following meanings:

(c) "Dwelling" includes, but is not limited to, any building, structure, vehicle, watercraft, or trailer adapted for human habitation actually lived in or reasonably could have been lived in at the time of the fire or explosion and any building or structure within the curtilage of that dwelling or that is appurtenant to or connected to the dwelling.

(d) "Building" includes any structure regardless of class or character and any building or structure within the curtilage of that building or structure or that is appurtenant to or connected to the building or structure.

W. 7ᵗʰ Raintree Ave.

Elsie Davis enters through the back attic window. She balances herself on a tight awning because she is trying to get to the chimney. Her friends are below her and they are silent. The sky is several shades of black with large clouds covering the moon so the light is just enough. They clip in a circle, drawing numbers with the toes of their shoes: four and snuffing it out with their heels, seven and snuffing it out with their heels. They make a tic-tac-toe board and with sticks begin to play.

There are not many differentiating ways to set something on fire. All you ever need are the proper conditions in which to make fire happen, Elsie Davis thinks to herself. *To make fire happen on a grand scale, the proportions have to be more exaggerated, and for a smaller scale, less drastic measures taken. I prefer gasoline and matches, those are my favorite.*

Gretchen Steinberg was brutally assaulted and the group of boys accused got off. They are quietly nesting in their parents houses, as none of them are over the age of eighteen, and none of them were convicted of anything.

In this beautiful house on the lake is Peter McArthur, the main suspect, the ringleader. You can hear the waves from outside, as if they are coming in, as if they are going to take the entire house away. Peter grew up in this house, had lived here his entire life, he never even had a different bedroom, Elsie Davis can point out his bedroom from the street. The house is calm. The water outside, she is angry, and rightfully so, so much poison in her body.

She crouches down outside of the window, a sprawling estate on one level.

Normally Elsie Davis can hear the *chug-glug* of the can as it hiccups, but tonight the lake is talking too much. She is nervous, even though weeks have gone by between the first two fires she knows she has to be careful. *Chug-glug*. She fights the instinct to clear her throat. She puts her hand up to her neck and swallows hard, thinks about Gretchen, grips the can tighter. When she has walked all the way around the house, she steps back and whistles to her friends. Each of them go to a different side, light matches, and hustle as fast as they can up a sand dune. The house goes so quickly, so much faster than the last one, and Elsie Davis is taken aback a bit by the velocity of the flame.

25 Hanyon Coaling Ave.

Elsie Davis takes her boyfriend, Salty, to this address. Salty rides a BMX bike, puts her big frame on the handlebars, slowly, steadily pushes the pedals until they are here, a house like all the rest of the houses in the only subdivision in town. The houses are huge and dark wood. The subdivision is disconnected and reconnected by two separate roads going in and out in a loop and attached at end by a lake inlet clean enough for the kids of the subdivision to swim in.

Elsie Davis knows one of Gretchen Steinberg's parents lives or lived here once, but does not quite remember where or which one.

One year, at the end of the school year, on the last half day of school when it is weird because it is only three hours and you don't really do anything but like laugh with your friends and eat food maybe and joke with your teachers or whatever, Elsie Davis asked Gretchen's older sister for a ride home and she reluctantly gave it to her.

9393 Palisades Road

Elsie Davis is in the woods crashing her body into Nathan's body and feels terrible about it because of Salty but does not stop. This house is gated. They jumped the gate. Nathan successfully covered up the one known camera at the rickety entrance. Two hops and they were over, on the property, through the creek-river, over the hills, into the trees.

Elsie Davis used to spend a lot of time at this house, two previous owners ago. The first owner built it from the ground up, friends of her parents, and then when they sold it, they sold it to Elsie Davis's crush's parents. She would have her friends drive cars down the street with their lights off, their music up so her crush could hear the bass lines, know it was her. She would call the house phone numerous times, until her crush's mother would yell at her to stop calling or else.

But her crush had long since not been her crush, his parents moved, and now the house is empty save for random tenants her long time ago crush's parents allow to live there.

She remembers being very drunk in that house the one and only time she made out with her crush on her crush's parents' bed. She remembers her crush telling her her boobs were "too squishy" for him, she was "too big" for him. It is a painful memory. Why does she even remember that? She is constantly confused at what she remembers and what she doesn't.

She will speak to this crush again, after many years have passed, through the Internet, and he will be as cruel as ever, maybe even crueler as an adult, will want to make sure she remembers all the terrible parts of herself which he remembers. All he will remember are the terrible parts.

She decides to not set this particular house on fire, even though she knows she should. She decides it is nice to be on Nathan's chest, looking through the tops of the pines, up at the sky.

2 Sahara Lane

Elsie Davis understands jealousy. She understands wanting.

Her old best friend Bobbi Jo decided she no longer wanted to be friends with her. She no longer wanted her around. Bobbi Jo decided to have a boyfriend, but Bobbi Jo always has a boyfriend, and they are always a parade of idiots, one right after another, with floats and hats and banners, we are idiots, yes we are. Sometimes they were run-of-the-mill small town idiots, the ones who drive huge trucks and do burn-outs on the high school front lawn. But sometimes, sometimes they were a special kind of idiot who hit her or told her she was fat and no one would ever love her. Those kinds of idiots were always the one she liked the best and she would use the word *love*, she *loved* those idiots, they were always the ones, too, who brought her flowers or wrote her gross rhyming poetry or took her out. One idiot, in particular, lost his virginity to her and then called Elsie Davis before school to cry about the fact that Bobbi Jo had already moved on to another boyfriend, What Did I Do to Deserve This? I Love Her, Elsie, I Love Her I Was a Good Boyfriend To Her. The intensity was so much she remembers crying, moved to tears by this idiot who actually thought Bobbi Jo loved him.

Bobbi Jo was nothing special, really, as far as Elsie Davis could ever see, except she was a very naturally small person, weight and height wise, very slight, and idiots went crazy for that, the slightness of her. Elsie Davis never understood it—why slightness was so attractive. Bobbi Jo was not particularly smart or funny or interested in much of anything, she wore oversized clothing and mostly tried to disappear and all of these idiots loved it. They also loved that she ate all the time—they loved feeding her. It was almost an experiment for some of them, to see if she would become bigger, and she never did, and she was always awarded for it somehow.

None of those idiots ever gave Elsie Davis a second look, none of them ever wanted her around unless she could do something for them. They never wanted to get to know her and all they did was treat Bobbi Jo badly or were so boring they didn't know how to treat her badly so Bobbi Jo got rid of them before they figured out that that is how she best related to the world, being treated badly.

If you look inside Bobbi Jo's family, as Elsie Davis is doing right now, outside of Bobbi Jo's house, you can see the pattern Bobbi Jo has followed, the reason why all the idiots in the idiot parade were always marching incorrectly to the beat outside of her body, or inside of her body, or through her body down the middle of it like a street. Elsie Davis sees Bobbi Jo's mom and her sisters, this long lineage of the same behavior, what idiot when, what love can find me where.

When Bobbi Jo has a boyfriend, she ignores Elsie Davis and when Bobbi Jo doesn't, she cannot leave her side. She never admits she cannot be alone. "Will you sleep in my bed with me, Elsie?" Bobbi Jo asks, and Elsie Davis

always does because she cannot help it. She wishes Bobbi
Jo didn't need a boyfriend all the time. She wishes she,
Elsie Davis, was enough.

This is a time of year when Bobbi Jo absolutely has a
boyfriend, he is of the first kind of idiot, the idiot she
will get rid of soon. For now, it is July and he is blonde
and dark skinned and laughs often and wants to go to the
beach every day and Bobbi Jo in her pink, plaid bikini
says yes to this and has no time for Elsie Davis.

She is watching Bobbi Jo through Bobbi Jo's bedroom
window and Bobbi Jo is bent over the side of her bed,
what is she up to, Elsie Davis does not want to wait to
find out. She sprays the stove fluid onto the back deck of
the house, lights a few matches, backs up to watch it burn
from the road.

STATE PENAL CODE (Excerpt)
Chapter XX
Arson & Burning

Section X00.110   Definitions

Sec. 110.
Unless the context requires otherwise, the following terms have the following meanings:

(e) "Damage", in addition to its ordinary meaning, includes, but is not limited to, charring, melting, scorching, burning, or breaking.

4 Larry River Road

Gretchen Steinberg's funeral was last night and Elsie Davis cannot stop thinking about her. She is standing in the tree line detaching Chad Bison's property and the beginning of an "in-road," or paved roads not close to the lakeshore. Chad Bison was co-ringleader next to Peter, but not smart enough to execute anything so violent on his own. In middle school, on the way to the bus one day, she saw Chad being bullied by his own brethren, they were calling him a pussy, calling him a girl. Those kind of insults always irked her—what was wrong with pussy? Why was calling someone a girl an insult? Because it's not an insult, dumbasses, she whispers under her breath. She has decided to set fire to all of the cars and motorcycles in the long driveway.

Amber is Chad's girlfriend and Amber is also in this house right now, her red Jetta parked next to Chad's bike. Amber and her family survived the fire in her home but were displaced during the re-construction and so Amber stays with Chad.

The sky is pink, the clouds are stratus, rising, so far away from her. It is daylight. Elsie Davis doesn't even want to wait until dark. She kicks over the two motorcycles closest to her, one heavy body humpf-ing onto the heftier body of the other and starts there with Zippo lighter fluid she stole from the gas station. She has twelve bottles in her backpack.

Old Hullberry Lane

There is a rumor a doll will appear under the old twisted oak tree at the end of this Lane, and once it appears you are being summoned for a game of hide-and-seek with the devil. If you lose, you go straight to hell, but if you win. No one has ever said what happens if you win. It is always assumed you will lose.

"Do you think we could set the entire woods on fire?" Octavia asks, while they are walking around the perimeter on the paved road, peeking through the chain-link fence.

Elsie Davis mulls this over. Would the doll appear? Would the doll burn? Will the whole town be sent to hell? Then it would be her fault the entire town is sent to hell. There are some good people in this town or at least old grandmas like her own who do not deserve to be sent to hell.

"I don't know, I don't wanna, too much work," Elise Davis says unconvincingly to Octavia.

STATE PENAL CODE (Excerpt)
Chapter XX
Arson & Burning

Section X00.110   Definitions

Sec. 110.
Unless the context requires otherwise, the following terms have the following meanings:

(f) "Physical injury" means an injury that includes, but is not limited to, the loss of a limb or use of a limb; loss of a foot, hand, finger, or thumb, or loss of use of a foot, hand, finger, or thumb; loss of an eye, ear, or loss of use of an eye or ear; loss or substantial impairment of a bodily function; serious visible disfigurement; a comatose state that lasts for more than three days; measurable brain or mental impairment; a skull fracture or other serious bone fracture; subdural hemorrhage or subdural hematoma; loss of an organ; heart attack; heat stroke; heat exhaustion; smoke inhalation; a burn including a chemical burn; or poisoning.

1224 Samantha Drive

Nina lives here and Elsie Davis is trying to figure out whether she wants to set the house made of huge stones on fire or not, if it would even burn. She can't decide.

Nina is a self-proclaimed witch, she wears a pentagram around her neck, keeps an altar in the rafters of the pole barn behind her parents' house. She attempted to initiate Elsie Davis long ago into a coven she called The Sisters of Darkness. She had business cards made up with her name and Elsie Davis's name and the names of two other girls she did not know, with a phone number. When she and Elsie Davis went to do a spell together, Elsie got so uneasy she threw up in the hay next to Nina's scrying mirror. This was the end Elsie Davis's time in The Sisters of Darkness.

The last time she hung out with Nina, Elsie Davis got to Nina's house and Nina was locked in her mother's bedroom with someone. When she knocked on the door, Nina told her she could either come in and join or go away. Elsie Davis got all hurt and left, not to see Nina again until Nina showed up out of nowhere to Elsie Davis's house to get her White Zombie t-shirt back. She sat on Elsie Davis's bed and told her a weird story about how when Elsie Davis got there, Nina had just gotten into the shower with her boyfriend because she had put chocolate syrup on him and licked it off because it was there, both the boyfriend and the chocolate syrup. Her boyfriend, Elsie Davis came to find out, was named Leopard, lived in the back of his Suburban, worked at a local misman-aged health food store, which Nina informed Elsie Davis that she would be working at, as well. At the time, Elsie Davis remembers feeling ashamed, of herself for some reason, of her body taking up so much space, of not be-ing cool enough to think of pouring chocolate sauce on someone, but now she feels rage at Nina for making her feel that way, rage at Nina calling her a "fat ass" because she thought her t-shirt was stretched, and rage at Nina thinking she was so much better than her with her White Zombie witch bullshit and her boyfriend named after a jungle cat.

All of this thinking cleared her head, she decides *yes, the front hedges will light.*

5 Maryland Drive

This is the circus train fire cemetery from the circus train fire that nearly wiped this town clean out years ago. The town was so decimated it was left off maps for a while.

You are greeted at the gates by two elephants, one with its trunk up and one with its trunk down.

Beyond the granite obelisk walls, the entire space is centered around the elephant. So many stories about the elephant: when the elephant was incinerated, the other elephants held trunk to tail and created a circle around the body, not allowing humans to reach their matriarch. At night they mumbled and trumpeted all night long. It took having to remove the other elephants for a human to be able to get close enough to her. No one could move her. It was decided to leave her there and construct a monument around her.

Headstones of trainers, of tamers, of freaks, of animals; concrete balloons, concrete acrobats in a 20 foot statuary surrounding the concrete remains of the keeper of the lions. Here lies Baldy the Clown. Here lies Frank the Bearded Lady. Here lies Marguerite and Mani, the conjoined twins.

Elsie Davis and her friends would skip school and laze amongst the granite and concrete, get high, stay all day. Octavia always said she felt the safest near the circular center of Big Mama the Matriarch Elephant, but Elsie liked slipping her feet in the concrete clown shoes near Baldy's grave the best.

.

001-007 The Arcades

Any major community activity happens inside the circus train cemetery. Every celebration of any major holiday, the human nativity scene at Christmas, the big Easter hunt for the kids, fireworks, it all goes down in the circus train cemetery.

The Arcades is the second ventricle to the heart, to the east of the cemetery, a small covered walkway on only one side of the street featuring a hair salon, a pizzeria, a grocery store, a post office, a general practitioner medical doctor, a pharmacy, and a fire station. Down the street on the other side is the gas station.

"During the next parade, let's set fire to the pharmacy," Elsie Davis says to herself as she huffs from the doctor's to the pharmacy to the grocery store for her grandmother.

753 2ⁿᵈ Street

From the roof of this house, you can see everything happening in the circus train fire cemetery.

You can see the Christmas lights never removed from one of the clown statue graves, making the entire stone blink and glow.

From the roof of this house, Octavia and Elsie Davis drink from a stolen bottle of vodka and whisper about how to ambush the cemetery. They have a plan to set fire to the graveyard—really let people in this town know they mean business.

"With all of the electricity up in there, it will blow right off the ground," Octavia says to Elsie Davis and Elsie Davis laughs louder than she should. Octavia cups her hand around Elsie's mouth and shushes her. She pushes Octavia hard away from her, takes another long drink from the bottle, wipes her mouth with the back of her hand.

18 Wellworth Pointe Drive

Salty tries to break up with Elsie Davis because he thinks he knows what is going on and he doesn't like it.

"It started as a prank but it's gone too far, Elsie, you are out of line completely," he says. They are parked behind the mausoleum in the circus train fire cemetery in Salty's dad's car getting high because all Salty has is a BMX bike and he pawned it the other day in the city for money he blew on video games and weed, which is at least what he told her, anyway.

Not that Elsie Davis ever believed a word he said.

"No, no, no," she says, "No, no, no." She is shaking her head left and right, and then up and down. What is yes and what is no? Is she saying no or yes?

She pulls out a knife from her crocheted, lacy purse and holds it up to Salty's throat.

"What the—hey, Elsie," he says. She doesn't stop and holds it so hard Salty coughs.

"No," is all she says.

002 The Arcades

Part of The Arcades is situated on the Circle Side and a part is situated on the Square Side as the town is divided into Circle and Square.

The rivalry of the Circles and Squares dates back to after the circus train fire. Those who didn't leave, even after the voluntary and involuntary evacuations, could not agree on which side of the freshly erected cemetery the new town should be on so, the division.

The division is stupid and Elsie Davis loves the graffiti, takes daily pictures of "Fuck Squares" and "Circles Suck Dick." Something goes up and then gets blocked out in white or black paint by the owners of the building and then something new goes up from the opposite group. One would think the small strip of storefronts would invest in both cameras and security systems but they don't. "The power of believing in honesty," says Elsie Davis to no one while she takes yet another picture of neon orange spray paint that reads "Die Squares" with what she believes is supposed to be a knife but looks like a bright orange cloud blob with a rectangle like a tumor under it.

Elsie Davis's grandmother is a die-hard Square. She often uses derogatory language against the Circles. "Those circles shouldn't even be here, they should be rounded up and shot."

"Grandma!," Elsie Davis says.

"Well…" her grandmother says, in a tone suggesting grandmother is surprised Elsie is surprised she would say something like that, a tone suggesting it is the truth, you young thing, listen all the way up.

42 Nottingwood Ave.

Nottingwood Ave. is the main road out to the highway, still half pavement. There is nothing on Rottingwood, as Elsie Davis calls it, except broken down billboards made of wooden slats advertising a motel that is no longer in existence, each advertisement letting you know how close you are getting to the motel, 1 ½ miles, ½ mile, ¼ of a mile, you are there! But it never arrives to you, you could drive up and down, back and forth, and never find it.

Elsie Davis wants to burn down the billboards. *No one would ever miss them and they aren't doing anything but taking up space. And who cares if the dead grass surrounding it burns, too. No one. No one cares. Let's burn it all down, from the highway to the circus train fire cemetery, let's set everything on fire.*

#1, Cynthia Street

Playground attached to a catholic church where it is reported the last priest molested a bunch of altar boys, classic story. The Archdiocese from the biggest city in the state stripped him of his title and he was forced to rehabilitate in an apartment in a smaller city so he could be close to this town because he was married and had seven children. The ex-priest terrorized his family, threatened suicide if his wife divorced him or slept with other people, accused her of sleeping with other people already, threatened to kill the children in their sleep. She eventually stopped taking his calls, stopped responding to his emails, stopped interacting with him in any way. The last phone call she received was from a social worker telling her he had drunk anti-freeze mixed with Tang and killed himself. He didn't actually want to die, or at least was not trying to intentionally kill himself all the way, just wanted to attempt, and that attempt, unfortunately, went very wrong.

The largest toy on the playground was mostly made of plastic and wood and so Elsie Davis started there first, gas and a stolen pack of matches from Bobbi Jo's house she had put in a scrap book she found again a few days ago; the pack had Big Al's Bar & Grill scrawled in terrible dripping blood font like a horror film—a steakhouse, primarily, with Tex-Mex and fried chicken thrown in. Elsie Davis hoped beyond hope the matches would light and when they did, she screamed out loud in joy.

Turtle Creek Beach

So many beaches, this one is by far Elsie Davis's favorite. She and Octavia and Brewer are sitting around in their underwear having just jumped in the water and they are simultaneously shivering and sweating when Elsie Davis comes across a turtle that is bleeding from its head, clearly a BB shot. She finds the round copper balls beyond the turtle's head. Turtle Creek Beach is now no longer her favorite. In fact, she never wants to come back here again. She wants to light whoever shot the turtle on fire.

99 Jerico Loop

Elsie Davis and Nathan are making out in the back of Nathan's truck and the curved metal of the truck bed is digging into Elsie Davis's back. She gets on top of him and he reaches up, grabs her breasts, her rounded stomach fat, wriggles up face as if smelling something bad, says "Your titties are too saggy, there's nothing to them," pushes her off. Embarrassed, she gathers herself, making the truck bed bounce. "Fuck you," she says under her breath. "I want to go home," she says. Nathan obliges her and they do not speak until

6701 Buell Street

Until Elsie Davis runs into Nathan at a party across town at a mutual friend's house. After a couple of beers she finds the nerve to say,

"Hey, what's up,"

and Nathan refuses to make eye contact.

"What are you doing here?" he asks.

There is a girl next to him she recognizes but doesn't know. The girl is tiny with bleach copper hair because her hair is so dark true blonde won't happen, a black velvet choke chain with a metal rose pendant hanging from the middle, a chevron patterned bikini top with an oversized black tank top over it.

"Can I talk to you?"

"No."

Elsie Davis looks at the floor, ceiling, bites her lower lip until it bleeds so she doesn't start to cry.

"I'm going outside," the girl she recognizes but doesn't know says to Nathan while giving her a sad, pathetic look, *poor stupid fat girl what is she even thinking?*

Nathan watches the girl step out the sliding glass doors

near them and looks Elsie Davis in the eyes.

"Look, leave me alone. Whatever happened was a fluke thing. I am trying to get with Koharu-Mei tonight, alright?"

Whispers: "I'm sorry but you are gross."

Loudly: "So stop trying to talk to me OK? God, I don't like you."

3333 Aiden Terrace

Elsie Davis starts with the back deck area which has a Hawaiian theme. Nathan's parents are renown for their tiki parties and the backyard is always set for a party.

She pulls all of the decorations off of the enclosed fence area, cut outs of ukuleles and hula-dancers. There has to be at least one hundred of them and she carries armloads, piling them in front of the door leading to the backyard. She stealthily douses the entire two tier deck in gasoline, three cans from Nathan's parents' shed and two cans she clumsily brought with her.

Once that is done, she hops the fence, throws all the unlit tiki torches over with her. She lights each one individually and throws them like a javelin back over the fence and into the yard. She watches the first one as it hits the edge of the stairs, it makes her heart jump, makes her palm sweat like she is kissing. She throws the rest of them, one right after the other—whoosh—whoosh—whoosh.

She runs to a very small patch of trees the alleyway behind Nathan's house to watch the entire back of the house. This is the best part, the watching. It is so beautiful and the beauty is what kills her the most.

997 Jug Factory Road

Fire makes me feel better, it calms me down, it allows me to control the outcome of everything and anything. The cursor is blinking, Elsie Davis stops writing. She is addicted to setting fires, it's the only thing making her feel OK anymore.

370 Liberty Court

Elsie Davis only babysat one time in her entire life, for a couple from her grandmother's church who had one baby.

To Liberty Court Elsie Davis went, her grandmother dropping her off. The night was normal, the baby was fine if not pleasant to be around, they had no real snacks or cable or Internet so it was just her and the baby.

Cut to: the couple pressuring her for sex. In the slyest way possible, the mother slipping her hands under Elsie Davis's skirt which she thought she had imagined, those hands up her skirt, the father cornering her in the kitchen.

She knew this is what was happening because it was obvious, but also because it was the only porno she ever watched with Nathan who wanted her to watch a 3:32 minute video of Couple Seduce Teen because the girl in the clip looked exactly like Elsie. Elsie Davis didn't believe him, of course, but then when they watched it, it definitely looked like her if she were to dye her hair red and curl it. The girl was husky like her, which is what she called herself, husky, like the boy's section in the old catalogues, but this girl had smaller boobs than Elsie Davis, which Nathan pointed out right away. Her jaw-line was square and Elsie Davis's wasn't. They immediately paused the video at 1:44 when the mother is making out with the teen and the father is taking the teen's pants off.

She did not care to see what happened next. They did an Internet search for stills or pictures of the old actress who played the teen and they found her on an obscure Swedish website that had many pictures of her in full latex cat-suits. The porn star's face was so similar to hers it was eerie, right down to the indent in the chin that made Elsie Davis's chin look like a butt.

Elsie Davis knew this couple was trying to have sex with her and she refused both of them. She asked to call her grandmother and she fake did, fake said grandma was on her way, fake said she was going to wait outside in the dark in their front lawn much to their dismay. She instead walked home, it started to a rain a little, a mist that did not leave her bones even after she got home, took a shower, finally got in bed.

8900 Circle Road

Koharu-Mei lives on this road with her humongous family in a humongous house right on the lake with private beach front access.

Koharu-Mei goes to private school and drives a brand new Audi, as does the rest of her brothers and sisters, they do not car pool.

Koharu-Mei looks so good in a bikini, which Elsie Davis will never be able to wear.

Elsie Davis wore a bikini once in middle school when she was running five miles a day into the woods far away from her grandmother's house to smoke exactly three Camel Wide Light cigarettes. Her grandmother was convinced that she was doing it to get fit and applauded her efforts, cascaded her with compliments. After she would spend the morning smoking, she would come back and lay out in a pink halter hand-me-down. That was the first and last summer of Elsie Davis's life that she wore a bikini.

Koharu-Mei lives in a bikini in summer and Elsie Davis, now knowing who she is, sees her at the gas station with all of her equally as beautiful and skinny friends who have dark skin and dark hair. Koharu-Mei has a summer uniform: oversized tank top and very small cut-off shorts that make Elsie Davis sink into her skin.

Elsie Davis is going to set Koharu-Mei's Audi on fire.

17 Middleboro Street

17 Middleboro Street is the last cabin on a tiny dirt road in the middle of nowhere very far away from where Elsie Davis and her friends live. This is where Salty presently lives. Salty always has a new place to live. Salty calls her, asks for a ride into town and she obliges, tells him to be outside when she pulls up. Salty is sitting on the grass with his bare feet up on a cement block and he is wearing a green, zip-up hoodie he has not taken off all summer and swimming trunks, a long toothpick hanging out of his mouth.

"You want your hoodie back?," he says to her while putting his hand through the passenger's side window and unlocking the door's lock by hand.

Salty stinks and so does the hoodie.

"Um, no, thank you, it's yours now, it's disgusting."

Salty laughs.

They pull out onto Middleboro Street and she does a U-turn.

"Hey, you didn't even look! Somebody could have been coming! And they would have hit my side!"

There is not another car out here for miles.

5542 Faith Street

Salty wants to rob the next house before Elsie Davis burns it. "Can I be in on a new house with you? I know you are still doing that shit. It's all in the paper and on the news. Don't lie about it, let me in on it, Els—"

He trails off and Elsie says "Fine," says "Yes," says "Don't tell the police anything if they ever ask you, promise," and they pinky swear on it, kiss the ends of their hands, wave them like wings, flap, flap. "Promise," Elsie says, "and you better fucking keep it."

Later, they are outside of 5542 Faith Street and it is a quiet, A-frame, three bedroom house with huge rooms and ceilings, a garage. They go to this address because Salty says, "There is money in this house, this is the house, there is money here."

"How do you know?," Elsie knows better than to question, Salty wouldn't be so specific if he wasn't confident.

"I know because this dude is the main contractor where I am working right now. He brags about the amount of cash in his place, I heard him the other day like a dickweed. You stay here."

Elsie stays crouched down like always, but she sits on the ground with her legs crossed because she knows she isn't going anywhere anytime soon. She wonders why Salty didn't care or wasn't concerned with the fact that she might tell on *him*, nevermind Salty telling on her. He wasn't even thinking about what if something on his end went wrong, as if nothing ever goes wrong for him, as if his execution is flawless.

She sees the lights in the house go on in the upstairs, she hopes the police aren't called.

She has no idea how much or how little time passes before a dark-figured Salty darts through the front door, across the lawn, grabs her up off the ground by the shirt, then by her hand and runs: and they run and run and run.

STATE PENAL CODE (Excerpt)
Chapter XX
Arson & Burning

Section X00.110   Definitions

Sec. 110.
Unless the context requires otherwise,
the following terms have the following
meanings:

(g) "Prior conviction" means a previous conviction for a violation of this
chapter that arises out of a separate transaction, whether under this
jurisdiction, a local ordinance substantially corresponding to this jurisdiction, a law of the United States
substantially corresponding to this
jurisdiction, or a law of another
state substantially corresponding to
this jurisdiction.

19900 Porterline Court

Salty and Elsie Davis are now sitting in the living room in a house of someone she does not know. Salty is dinking around on an iPad, he is checking his social media websites because he can, he says. Salty explains loudly after a few whiskeys he ransacked the house over on Faith Street, stole all this mother fucker's money and the iPad, which he proudly holds above his head. He says he had to tie the old people up and then there were kids in their bedrooms and the lady was begging saying that there were kids in the other room and she did not want the kids to see them like this and then the dude talked too much, Salty said, so he hit him with a vase, just broke a goddamn vase over this old dude's head and the lady screamed and he threatened to hit her too if she didn't tell him where their safe was and so that was that and here they are.

Some of the friends love this story and some of them do not love this story. One girl talks outside about how the gratuitous violence was unnecessary and how Salty always brings trouble and Elsie Davis only hears this because she is standing near the window in the kitchen nearest the back porch. She watches the june bugs fly into the flood light on the opposite corner of the porch, feels sick to her stomach, goes into the bathroom and dumps the packets of matches down the toilet, flushes it.

There is a knock on the door. One of the various blonde shaggy haired boys answers and then shuts it. Says, "Yo, it's a negotiator from the cop shop." All eyes on Salty.

"Whatta they want?" says Salty.

"They want you," the blonde boy says. "Where is Carl?"

Carl is the owner of the house. Carl is 6'11 with a sizable black beard and enormous black curly hair with tiny, tiny square framed glasses. He speaks softly and with a slight lisp. He is wearing overalls and nothing else and quietly crosses the living room, disappears out the front door.

When Carl comes back into the house, he tells everyone to go into the basement, including Salty. He grabs his gun and says, "Now this is a hostage situation, no one can leave and no one can come. Stop using your phones immediately." And, in two strides, he goes over to Salty and swats the iPad from his hands.

"They are here because of you," and Carl steps on the iPad, breaks its screen in a clean crack down the middle. "I have warrants so no one is leaving."

It is true, the police tracked Salty and Elsie Davis to Carl's house through the use of the stolen iPad.

Everyone is stuck in the basement. Salty increasingly becomes more sober. He starts pacing. Tanya and Bower, Salty and Carl's friends, have a baby at Bower's mom's and Tanya is getting upset Bower's mom will know something is up because they are not going to be there on time to pick up their baby and now Tanya is scared. No one has been scared yet but now Tanya is and it is upsetting. She is so upset Bower finally decides to go talk to Carl.

Carl allows Tanya and Bower to leave and this is a sign of good faith from Salty and Carl to the negotiator and the police. Salty goes upstairs with Tanya and Bower and comes back with another gun. There are now two loaded guns in plain view. Everyone else has to stay, including Elsie Davis. She doesn't speak to anyone and no one speaks to her. In fact, no one speaks to anyone else, everyone stares at the floor or closes their eyes or watches Salty pace and become increasingly more erratic.

Carl comes downstairs once Tanya and Bower have left and pleads with Salty to come clean, give himself up. It will be revealed later Carl and Salty already robbed 5542 Faith Street a week beforehand and had gotten away with it, or so it seemed at the time, but now that Salty was greedy the cops have more evidence and know for almost certain it was Carl and Salty the first time, which of course it is. We don't know this yet, we in the basement, but we watch as Carl tries to convince Salty of coming clean.
Salty keeps repeating the same thing over and over "I

can't go back to jail, man, I can't go back to jail, man, I can't go back to jail, man, I can't go back to jail." Not many people in the basement know Salty had just gotten out of a nine month stint in jail for violent assault, armed robbery, intent to kill. His parents hired the best lawyers on that side of the state, got him out of a third felony by pleading his insanity, he did a three month stay in a psychiatric hospital and jail time. After, his parents washed their hands of him, told him next time he goes to prison forever.

Carl talks Salty into going upstairs with him and he does.

The next thing anyone hears is what sounds and feels like a gunshot.

The police yell at everyone to put their hands in the air, usher them out of the basement, through the garage, and into the street where it is full-on daylight.

They search everyone and take their names down.

They search Elsie Davis, find nothing but her state ID and a pack of Juicy Fruit, she is so happy she flushed those matchbooks. One of the cops asks her if she is OK, makes a joke about having a rough night, winks at her, sends her on her way.

The cop, also, before sending her on her way, asks her questions about who she knew at the party, what she knew about the robbery, but she denies everything, said she went with a friend and the friend ditched her, which was partially true. She said she knew no one, not even Carl, was hoping to get a ride home from someone she overheard lived in her neighborhood down the way.

For two days straight, Elsie Davis doesn't leave her bed, tells her grandmother she has a fever, she needs a break. She is trying to avoid everything because she doesn't want to see the mug shots of Carl with no beard or hair and Salty with a multi-colored mohawk, which is on any screen she sees. Salty killed himself instead of going back to jail, Carl took the blame for everything—all of the break-ins, all of the robberies. The people on Faith Street recognized him as the other person who came with Salty the first time. The old man claims he recognized Salty immediately, too, whose legal name is not Salty, not that Elsie Davis ever thought it was.

0017 California Street

California Street, in the northwest part of town, is both the poorest and richest street. One half is made up of looming mansions set back from the road closer to the shoreline containing mostly seasonal residents, and one house owned by a B-list actor, someone buff and dumb who is a perpetual bachelor and this year's hottest panty-wetter by some stupid magazine.

The street splits at the other cemetery, Partridge Cemetery, a small but quaint place filled with oak trees, simple headstones as far as the eye can see, over the hill and down near the river. The headstone closest to the river has two huge hearts made of pink granite sticking out of a pedestal that says Our Divine Angel and some dates very close together; a little girl who was abducted, killed, left for dead in the woods of a county on the other side of the state by her best friend's father.

The street splits at the cemetery and then houses, one bedroom or no bedroom, one room and a kitchenette or no kitchenette, just a burner in the corner, everyone has a bathroom at least, no tub, standing shower, toilet, and filled to the brim with people, filled to the brim with yards full of metal and garbage.

Elsie Davis remembers coming to this part of California as a kid, before she moved in with her grandmother, because her parents owned a house not far from this lakeshore.

California Street is where most of Carl's possessions are, a 200 sq. foot "house" at the end of the street, the last one in front of the blueberry farm turned day camp for kids with cancer. Carl's baby mama told Elsie Davis and Octavia this when Carl's baby mama flopped herself over to Octavia's mom's apartment after Carl was arrested: that she had kicked him out a few days before "… and one of those stupid little houses were for rent so he called the guy and then that's where he was livin,' in a shack on the outskirts of town." She let him back in the night before it all went down but the majority of his stuff was still there, "it would be a shame if it all burned up wouldn't it?," Carl's baby mama asks.

4447 Fleischer Drive

The Most Beautiful Girl in the World lives in this house

and Elsie Davis ate psychedelics with her friends about

two hours ago and now she is standing at the end of a

private property beach, gazing at this gigantic mansion facing

the lake, it looks like it is going to fall forward,

should I tell them? *Should I tell everyone in the house*

wake up the front face of your house is going to fall into

the water and then what?

       Elsie Davis is getting

freaked out about every living creature in the water,

will they all be beached? Will I be the sole person

who has to take care of them? All she has is her ball cap,

will I have to fill my Detroit ball cap with water and

put it on the skin of creatures to make sure they don't dry out?

How will I protect them all? She is wringing her hands

and gliding up the sand, through the dune grass, closer to
the house.

The Most Beautiful Girl in the World must be sleeping

she says aloud, startled at her own voice. This girl

was the first person she ever kissed, the first person who
ever wanted

to kiss her, at a party in a pantry among cases

of bottled water, this girl pulled on the neck of her t-shirt

and kissed her, went upstairs and acted like nothing happened.

When Elsie Davis

asked her about it at school on Monday,

The Most Beautiful Girl in the World laughed in her face,

told her she was a loser, told her she was drunk and

thought Elsie Davis was a dude, "Oops sorry."

Should I set her house on fire?

she asks herself,

and giggles uncontrollably at first,

and then she thinks again, sits down in the sand, looks out,

into the full moon lake clouds perfect July night and says aloud

"I should, I should burn this girl's house down right now,"

begins to feel around her pockets for matches but has nothing with her,

giggles again, walks back to her friends.

01210 E. Normandy Ave./Egypt Tool

Salty's sister is letting Elsie Davis use his truck, a black Explorer XLT with a huge Grateful Dead sticker on the left back window, because she has no use for it and it is all paid up through September so why not, go ahead, don't get in trouble, wink and smile and here are the keys. Salty's older sister tells her she is the only girl Salty ever talked about in the last few years, Elsie Davis was extra special to her dumb-ass brother. Salty's sister is not one for emotions or small-talk, she says she is like a dude in that way and Elsie reminds her no, she is just like a person in that way, anyone can be any way they want and Salty's sister says, "You are so freewheelin' and that's why Salty loved you so much." She pauses after she says the word love.

She picks up Octavia and they go out to Egypt Tool, both a metal supply shop/factory and two track dirt road that leads to nowhere. They are going to sit in Salty's car and get high in honor of him.

They find a spot and nestle into the trees, roll down the windows, Octavia lights a cigarette when they hear a *bang bang bang* on the back of the car. Elsie Davis grabs the steering wheel, hands on key, ready to start the car when she looks in the rearview mirror and realizes it is a little girl.

Elsie Davis opens the door, "Hey, what are you doing out here?" she looks around, "Where are your parents at?"

The little girl is holding a doll in her hand and letting it drag in the mud.

"Where do you live?"

The little girl points to some patch of trees. By this time, Elsie Davis and Octavia are out of the car.

"You live in those trees?," says Octavia

The little girl shakes her head no.

"Will you take me to where you live?," Octavia holds out her hand, but the little girl backs away.

Elsie Davis says, "Look, baby, you better get on home, this is how kids get snatched up. You shouldn't be out here with nobody. Get on, now. Go."

The little girl looks at them, shakes the braids all over her head so her barrettes clink together because its obvious she just loves the sound because she begins to laugh, and takes off running in the direction of where Elsie Davis and Octavia saw her point to where she lived.

They get back in the car, and after twenty minutes have gone by, they both get out and go investigate where she said she lived to make sure she wasn't actually living back in the woods. They find nothing but another walking trail leading to the backs of a row of houses, still too far for a little girl to be by herself.

74 Sarasota Street

This is an empty lot with one burned out abandoned building and Brewer likes to park his car behind it and do target practice with a rifle. Octavia and I watch him *pingping* the cans until we are bored of laying on the hood of the car and watching the sky, it gets too hot this time of year, the hood burns our legs and arms, we always forget a blanket.

The building was once an historical attraction. Some famous old person was born there. In the circus train fire it burned up but the remnants stand. People still come to see it and take pictures even though it is just a hollow shell. It is here on the top of the hood that I decide no more fires, or we should move on to all the bigger buildings and structures we talked about, or move on to another town. I want to retire. My stomach is in knots just thinking about quitting.

Even though there are serious restrictions on guns allowed in the city limits, there is not one police officer in town who would abide by it. When the town once resembled a real place, before the circus train fire, maybe, but not now. The shots from the rifle are loud and no one complains.

Emergency/Non-Emergency Police/Fire
Scan

Overheard over Elsie Davis's grandmother's scanner:

"10-20, I am en route across the bridge
to see about a 10-58 (suspicious person) near the old cannery, was told
there may be an arson in progress. Je-
sus Christ, not another one."

8 Monte Vista, #9

In Octavia's mom's apartment, Octavia and Elsie Davis are sitting around listening to music, eating peanut butter and butter sandwiches and potato chips, drinking Diet Mountain Dew because it is all her mother drinks these days since she stopped drinking booze.

"I heard over the scanner last night someone was trying to set the old cannery on fire," Elsie Davis watches Octavia's face for any sign it might be her.

"Holy shit, why didn't you tell me you were goin' across the bridge?"

"No, it wasn't me! I swear, I was at home listening to the goddamn police scanner with my grandma, if I was going to start setting shit on fire across the bridge, number one I wouldn't start with the old cannery for christssake and for two I would be totally bringing you, come on.

"Dang," Octavia finally says. "A copy-cat fire-starter." She has a deathly serious face on, a tinge of almost sadness in her voice.

5331 Paul Konlon Street NE

The town a town away from Elsie Davis's town is not any bigger than Elsie Davis's town except it has less fire damage, but still some fire damage. The town a town away always wants to act as if the fire didn't effect them but of course it did, if anything lots of people decided to stay in the area just not in Elsie Davis's town so they moved into the town a town away. The town a town away is defined by food, but not good food, fast food that made people sick. It was the only town for miles with a gas station-Taco Shack-Pizza Palace-combo. She and her friends would sometimes drive from the beach directly to the town a town away to go to the gas station to eat; it was a highlight.

The town a town away is also defined by a large rumbling not felt on the other side in the other town a town away where Elsie Davis lives. It would begin at sunset and the ground felt as if it was opening up. Every house on a certain fault line, near the bridge, had to live a certain way so their things did not get shaken and broken, so they themselves did not get shaken and broken. Her town was always afraid of the bridge being severed.

Scientists from all over the world had come to the town a town away to see about this shaking at sunset and, while there are many theories, there is not one set conclusion, and the shaking continues. You get used to it after awhile, but it is the reason why Elsie Davis and her friends do not go there often.

The fires in the town a town away will begin during sunset, during the shaking. The first thing on fire is a house on Paul Konlon, near the high school. It is a ranch-style home, a refurbished barn, and the reasoning will be an electrical wire snapped during the trembling, which regularly happens, and fell on some trees, which then fell on the house.

Elsie Davis watches the fires on TV. She knows by the flames it is more than a downed wire. Someone is starting to set fires in the town a town away.

997 Jug Factory Road

It is 100 degrees out and Octavia, Brewer, and Elsie Davis are under a huge umbrella on the beach in front of Elsie Davis's grandmother's house. It is no cooler on the beach than in the house but at least there is a hot breeze once in a while outside. Elsie Davis has a black t-shirt on she has cut the neck out of so her shoulders are exposed and a pair of the shortest shorts she will allow herself, mid-thigh, exposing nothing. She doesn't have a bathing suit but a normal bra on. Octavia is dark skinned and has stretch marks coming off her thighs and on to her ass as if they are two hands clutching for eternity and the stretch marks are made more visible by the darkness of her skin. Elsie Davis loves those stretch marks and that ass—it is in a green one piece bathing suit that fits her perfectly. Her brother is in a green pair of cargo shorts, his boxer shorts up on his waist and his cargo shorts sagging well below them.

Three boys in striped swimming trunks and perfect chests pass them, throwing a ball among them and catching it and throwing it again to another person. Elsie Davis overhears their conversation: another set of houses in the town a town away were set on fire early this morning, on Rosalinda Court, a cul-de-sac of houses all the same, there are a lot of those in the town a town away. Two houses, side by side, as if kissing and holding hands, done from the bottom up, gardens first.

Elsie Davis shakes Octavia awake but Octavia is already

awake. They both look at each other knowingly through their sunglasses but neither of them move an inch until sunset.

88 Merwyn Woods

Elsie Davis gets a letter from Carl in prison Salty's sister gives her when she returns Salty's truck.

The letter says *I know you are setting those fires, but now you have competition. This is what you get for being a rat, here is your trap.*

There are some large portions blacked out, two whole pages of black. Carl clearly had something to get off his chest.

The back of the envelope has words in hand-drawn graffiti letters.

The words: "Always Remembering, Never Forgetting."

7171 Delaware Street

Elsie Davis had big plans to burn some of the larger abandoned buildings down, to burn the playground, to burn the school, she had big plans, huge plans, plans that kept her up at night scheming, drawing maps, which she is burning in the back of her house right now in grandmother's old yellow steel wheelbarrow, she has filled it with water with the hose first because she doesn't want to light her grandmother's house on fire and she briefly considers this, why it is OK for her to light other people's property on fire but it is not OK to light her grandmother's because her grandmother is old and she loves her but then a voice in her head intervenes and says *yes but some of those people were old and people loved them* and then Elsie slaps the side of her head with her open palm, brings herself out of the spiral. She drew maps to every single house, every structure, how to get there the best way on foot, in a car, going right up to the windows, up the roofs, up the trestles, on the stairs, on the decks, in the yards, on the roads, and she knew every measure, every foot, every yard, every minute, every second, she had it down to a science, the craft of setting fires. She is burning the evidence because she is scared. She is burning every map individually with a lighter, one of the cheap clear ones where you can set the setting high, the flame nearly setting the lighter itself on fire every time it is flicked. She is setting the end of the high flame to the lavender colored paper and burning all of the maps to everywhere. She was angry at first, and jealous, and now she doesn't want anything to do with it—burn the evidence, just in case. "I

am off fires for a while," she says to Octavia who knows
she is lying but what can she do.

33 ½ Jim Bob Way

Jim Bob and Margaret Griswalde live at the furthest point west possible until they are almost out of the county completely. They own 600 acres of land and Jim Bob still farms it every season but winter, when he takes a rest.

Jim Bob and Margaret Griswalde are Elsie Davis's grandmother's best friends for 45 years. They have known each other almost their entire lives.

Jim Bob and Margaret Griswalde live on a road called Jim Bob Way because the county road commissioner's office said Jim Bob and Margaret could name the dirt road their farm is on and give each little building a separate address if they so choose and Jim Bob did so choose and he named the road Jim Bob Way. He had an offensive joke about Zimbabwe he liked to tell and it always got a laugh out of the old white men standing around with hay in their mouths, which included Elsie's grandfather once a long time ago.

Jim Bob and Margaret Griswalde's address is so far off in its own territory that some buildings' addresses are listed as being in Elsie Davis's hometown and some are in the town a town away.

Jim Bob and Margaret Griswalde are found dead in a raging fire spanning four buildings and a silo. The most fantastic display yet, far out-staging anything Elsie Davis had ever pulled off. It made her terrified and delighted.

6931 Ruby Ave.

Another letter from prison, this time sent to Salty and Elsie Davis's mutual friend Annie.

The letter has less black-outs but the message is the same, *how do you like it, Elsie Davis you fucking bitch.*

9530 Tammy Drive

"He knows," is all Elsie Davis says to Octavia. They are sitting outside a soft-serv ice cream shop in a town next to the town a town away.

"He knows what? He don't know nothin'," Octavia says, licking dripping swirl off her hand.

"No, these letters though, he knows, dude, he knows, but I am done so I don't know what this is all about now. Should I go to the police?"

"Hell, no. Hell no. You go to the police, it will get worse, and you will be in trouble, you have zero alibi. What could you possibly even say? We will end up in so much trouble."

"We?"

"You will tell on me, its envitable."

Elsie Davis smacks the ice cream cone out of Octavia's hand and it lands at the feet of a small child who then tries to scoop some up with his fingers and his busy mother hits his hand for trying to scoop up the ice cream and he starts to cry. The mother picks him up, dries off his face, starts dancing around with him on her hip. Elsie Davis's eyes begin to well. She wants to run far, far away from here. Octavia won't look at her, doesn't look at her all the way home.

540 Cherry Blossom Ave. NE

The fires in the town a town away are getting closer to the bridge and it's making Elsie Davis nervous. The last one, three days ago, was reported on Cherry Blossom Ave NE and Elsie Davis is on the Internet mapping them all out, starting as far West as possible and going and going until. Too close for comfort, too close to home, who is next. She wants to believe the Griswalde's were a mere coincidence, but how is she supposed to know?

She has not spoken to Octavia since the ice cream incident and she feels awful about it, she has written her, on the Internet, called her, to no avail. Brewer once answered the house phone, and said she wasn't there but Elsie Davis was too pissed to ask anymore questions and hung up on Brewer while he was mid-sentence. She thinks he was going to ask how she was doing but like, how was she doing? She was doing horribly. *Look what I have done*, she thought, *look what I have started*.

It is the final weeks of July, she is so happy to have this month almost over. She hates July. She wants everything to go back to normal, to go back to school in the fall, to forget all of this has ever happened.

65 Hazel Drive

65 Hazel Drive is where the last remaining drive-in movie theatre is in the state and Elsie Davis is there to try to find Octavia and confront her about why she hasn't spoken to her in so long, the situation is in the past, Elsie Davis can't go back and put the ice cream back on her cone, stop that kid from crying, she can't change what had happened, she felt disrespected, and she knows that that is no way to act and Octavia knows how much she loves her, is obsessed with her, cannot see the next tomorrow without her, will you please talk to me, please talk to me.

When the movies begin, she sneaks around the cars, looking for Octavia, listening for her laugh, she gets through all three screens, doesn't find her. She is here on a rumor, their friend Cooter told her when she stopped at the gas station that is where she would be tonight on a date, *a date* Elsie thought at the time and still thinks, *a date, what does that even mean? Has Octavia ever been on a date before? And with who?* Whoever it is, she wants to burn his house down.

When Elsie Davis begins to walk away and make her way home, she thinks she hears the glint of Octavia's voice, the shadow of her walk, the way her hips move side to side, but it was not her, either time.

7757 San Juan Street

Elsie Davis takes her grandmother's Cadillac and drives to San Juan Street, on the corner of California and San Juan, right before it turns into shacks and garbage lawns.

Elsie Davis so far had only one more unrequited boy crush in her life, Maloney Bardicks. Maloney is much older than her, and Maloney was dating a friend of hers who is now no longer her friend. Elsie Davis tended to have a lot of those, friends who were not actually friends but were friends for while and now are no longer friends. Her whole life, in fact, was defined by those friends.

Maloney was different, he seemed smart and interested in books, movies, music, had wild green spiral curly hair he shaved into a mohawk, he wore purple Airwalks and he was Very. Cool. Elsie Davis didn't think Maloney should be with her friend because her friend was kind of ditzy and wasn't interested in anything. Her friend had nice tits, Maloney said, so nice, but that's about it.

Elsie Davis is sitting outside Maloney's parent's house in the car. She doesn't know what led her here to these memories. The urge to get out, spray that front screened-in porch with lighter fluid and set the whole thing on fire was so strong she has to physically swallow it down. She chokes on this feeling and doesn't know what to do, pulls out a lighter from the cup holder next to her and runs it over the underside of her hand, doesn't feel or smell the burn when it begins.

1 Dumpy Road

Elsie Davis's grandmother tells her someone tried to set the methane flame in the dump on fire in the town a town away. They were unsuccessful "...and thank the Lord because if they did the entire town a town away would have gone ka-blooey," her grandmother says.

99 John Stuart Preston Blvd NE

Octavia and Elsie Davis make up because they always make up. They are best friends again. It will only be a matter of time before they are not best friends anymore.

They hear about 99 John Stuart Preston Blvd over the police scanner and by the time they get there on Octavia's Honda NQ50 Spree she bought for $75.00 off of a neighbor who has a surprisingly curious and quiet meth habit (the guy works for the water department! has for twenty years!), there are so many people and so much commotion they keep on driving past, Octavia hunched over the top of the scooter, making it go as fast as it could go, and Elsie Davis behind her, holding on, arms folded over each other around Octavia's waist.

This house, a sprawling beach front estate with seven bedrooms, three and a half bathrooms, four stall garage, three sand dunes, three docks in the water, all of the dune grass one can stomach, was crumbling in flames. These are seasonal houses. Almost all of Elsie Davis's hometown's money comes from summer people. They need summer people. No summer people, the town is a goner. Luckily, no one was there right now, end of July, middle of summer. So. Lucky.

This one shook Elsie Davis to her bones. She could hear her blood, her temples were pounding. Despite the heat, her cheeks were cold, she was sweating. There could have been a family of like twenty in that house. She marveled, which she felt embarrassed by, at the handiwork displayed time and again by whoever was doing this. A massive house, a huge job. She wished they could have gotten closer to the scene, she wanted to scan the crowd so badly—who was it, she knew they were there somewhere.

997 Jug Factory Road

"The fire is coming over the bridge," Octavia says. They are watching TV with their feet up on the couch, they are lying side by side, feet to head and they are watching the local affiliate down by the water report on John Stuart Preston Blvd.

"This person is about to invade your territory," Octavia says.

After Octavia goes home, Elsie Davis is in her room alone. She is thinking about how the fire is coming back for her. How the fire knows what she has done and she thinks should *I go say sorry, should I apologize to everyone that I mistreated, that I hurt, that I burned, should I turn myself in, what should I do*. She has never had this kind of regret, guilt. It nagged at her, she turned over in her bed, felt a presence in the room, as if her guilt had personified and was sitting on her shoulder, or at the edge of her bed, or on the headboard looking outside the window. It is sitting outside of her, in the dark with her, saying *look how badly you messed everything up, you should be ashamed of yourself, you should turn yourself in for what you have done*. Elsie refuses to open her eyes, refuses to acknowledge it, tosses and turns it away until she finally falls asleep.

But it was still there, hunkered in a corner when she woke up, sun in her face, all the curtains open.

Everywhere she went, there it was.

"I thought you left already," she said aloud to herself walking down the street to The Arcades. She feels like she is cracking up.

8787 Washington Street

On a side street in the trailer parker, rain. Elsie Davis is there to pick up another letter from Carl. She is scared but there has been no more fires since the one on John Stuart Preston, the one so close to the bridge. She figured it was all done. She figured she had learned her lesson, even though she never did anything to Carl.

Last week she wrote Carl back after Salty's sister, after all of their friends, told her not to. Told him she never said anything to the police, said that she didn't know nothin' about the fires, didn't know nothin' about what happened that night with Salty, all she did was love that kid, what are you trying to do to me????

She tears open the envelope of the new letter:

Dear Elsie Davis,
See you in hell,
Carl

4353 Lincoln Street

She tries another trailer, now determined to figure out who is setting these fires for Carl, how to stop them.

How to stop them, she can stop them, she started them and now she can stop them.
How to stop them, how to stop them, she can stop them, how to stop them.

She unravels on her friend at this trailer who does not know Salty, does not know Carl, barely knows Elsie Davis, and Elsie Davis tells her everything, from start to finish, "What do I do what do I do, how do I find this person, what do I do?" and the friend offers no help, has a baby in the other room who starts to cry. "What do I do what do I do?

"Maybe you should just go to the pol,"—her friend trails off before her head hits her chest, mouth open, drooling.

Elsie Davis stomps her feet, claps her hands together hard in front of her friend's face, says, "Hey, hey, hey, wake the fuck up dude your baby is crying."

Her friend mumbles, "Oh, she will be fine, it will just be for a minute,"

Her friend starts to bleed from her nose.

Elsie walks to where the baby is crying, who is standing

at the edge of crib, covered in shit from belly-button to ankle. The room is sweltering, no fans, and no windows.

Her friend eventually comes to and doesn't have a lot to say. Cleans up in the bathroom, takes care of the baby, begins to give it a bath in the dirty dishwater in the sink in the kitchen. Elsie Davis leaves.

997 Jug Factory Road

Octavia and Elsie Davis are no longer best friends, this time forever.

No one will talk to Elsie Davis anymore and there are no more letters.

The phone does not ring and no one comes to her grandmother's door.

The final days of July end with fireworks being set off by neighborhood boys

because the laws have been lifted, now you can get anything you want.

"It is a firework state," says one of her neighbors to her grandmother when

they are outside sitting in the shade and drinking tea together, not speaking.

Her grandmother doesn't have much to say these days either, says she has

practically said everything she needs to say, tells the same stories over and

again. The final days of July and finally Elsie Davis is calm, no longer has to worry about Carl or Salty or anyone else. A firework goes off in the distance,

bang pop. High pitch whiz pop. Popopopop. "Sounds like artillery," says her grandmother

who served in the army. "Yes, ma'am, it does," says Elsie. "Artillery, indeed."

6100 Old Zion Baptist Road

Overnight, there is another fire.

It has crossed the bridge.

It is in her town.

She did not do it.

An old house on the edge of the circus train fire cemetery.

The fire was about to go over the stone wall when it was finally put out.

Here it is.

It is here.

What to do, what to do.

Elsie Davis catches a glimpse of herself in a tinted window of an unmarked cop car at the

scene. She has the darkest circles under her eyes, like she has been beaten.

55 Elihue Street

Elsie Davis slept in the circus train fire cemetery because she wanted to be the closest to the new fire, she wanted to smell the smoke and see the flames being doused, she wanted to see the spectacle and watch for anyone who might be suspect. The same old crowd showed up, the same neighbors and the same children and the same fire-fighters. This was their day off someone told someone else. The firefighters working on their day off for a fire not set by her in her town, she was furious. No one looked out of place. The fire was put out in an hour or so, *due to high winds, when the winds pick up they can't continue to try to put the fire out, they have to wait, it becomes dangerous, not that it wasn't before, but a greater risk*, this is what she is thinking about, yes, *a greater risk to bodily harm, to safety, and the wind dies down and they put it out* and now she is lying between the large headstones of Kona and Kora Merriweather, The Largest Little Women in All The World their head-stones read and there is just enough room between them for Elsie Davis's entire body so there she is, nestled in the granite bosoms of Kona and Kora.

In the daytime, when the heat and humidity is still kind of low, she creeps over the stone fence and up to the damp majestic house. It didn't even look like the same place, they never do, their faces all scarred, distorted. That's the thing about fire, you can't just repair most of the time, you have to rebuild, if you want no indication the fire had happened, and with one like this, there is no way to recover with no signs of damage. She swore she could still hear the hiss whistle of the fire settling into the wood like a cold in bones, she swears she could feel the heat radiating off it, beyond the yellow caution tape, the sign declaring the police and the firefighters had been there, to stay away, and anyone who knows anything about anything CASH REWARD in huge blue letters, CASH REWARD.

There is a certain smell to house fire smoke in particular that cannot be replicated. It comes from patina and antiques and memories and years. It comes from collecting, all of your things, feelings, people. Who actually cares about that Christmas card, the only one you ever received from your father when he was deployed and never came home? Who cares about all 500 of your very rare records (How did you eat the summer you bought those? What did you eat that summer? Did you eat that summer?) No one but you, maybe a hand full of other people not including the insurance people and the estimation people and the restoration people, etc, and even to those people, who cares about your stuff? It's all just stuff anyway. A house is a thing you live in, a dwelling. A dwelling is a place where you store your stuff, and if you lose that? You are only losing a dwelling and things, right? Memories, trinkets, objects, who cares? A smell that only happens when the memories and trinkets are burned? By a flame of oranges, yellows, blues, you can feel the blues. How does time smell on fire?

5 Watermelon Beach Road

Watermelon Beach is Elsie Davis's new favorite beach; a beach given its name due to the chemical plant down the road dumps all of its waste into that part of the lake, part of the lake funneled to this part where the children would swim and the mothers would eat or read magazines or both, listen to the radio if they had one. The children would carry plastic shopping baskets into the water with them if they knew to go deep enough and where, they could bring up baskets full of clams, the shells iridescent and rainbow streaked. They would drag in the baskets and crack open the valves, throw whatever half contained the most gunk and keep the other half, washing it in water and bringing it to the mothers. The children still did that and Elsie watched them as they did it.

These waters are not safe, however, and that is why she refuses to go in, she just wants to sit next to it with her book and her worries. The state has said you can get chemical burns spending too much time in these waters and all of the families today are migrant families who do not speak English or very little or simply don't want to speak it today or around her. She catches bits of Spanish here and there, what she can remember from freshman Spanish, I'm sorry and thanks and My God and that's about it.

One family is listening to the local top 40 radio station and playing volleyball. One of the boys likes the song, turns the radio up, and the song is interrupted with an announcement that another fire has been reported near Westdale Street and 23rd in her town—which is just a little ways away. The family keeps playing volleyball. The boy seems annoyed his song was interrupted. No one gets out of the water or calls their children in. No one seems to care.

On the Corner of Westdale and 23rd

Seventeen acres of dark undeveloped trees and grass are on fire.

There has been a report, a large man with dark hair and dark eyes and dark skin

and here is the composite some person drew

and the police are there handing out fliers to the same crowd as ever,

only this time Elsie Davis is standing in the crowd, shoulder to shoulder with

her neighbors, and she gets a flier and stares at the drawing

No it could not be

Not it could not be

Impossible it could not possibly be

170 Kennedy Street

This dumb girl Elsie Davis has to go see about right now has a letter from Carl, the fourth and final one. She does not know how this dumb girl knows Carl or how Carl knows this dumb girl. She is tired of these letters and she is tired of having to retrieve them.

This girl, with her mousy brown hair and blue streaks, this girl, says to her, "Stay outside."

It is over 100 degrees today, humid, one more day of July left before August can be ushered in with the fall. Elsie Davis greets it, wants it, needs it. She is over it. Elsie Davis can see at least three window unit air conditioners hanging out the gaping windows of the trailer and it makes her mad she has to stay outside.

One last letter: *It's over.*

Elsie Davis tears the envelope open, reads the letter, tears it up into as tiny of pieces as her thick fingers can muster, and throws it on the ground at the girl's feet. Elsie Davis turns and walks away. She is no longer afraid of anything.

1032 West Virginia Road

Until, she gets back to her grandmother's house, and on
the south side of her lawn,
in her neighbor's yard,
all of the overgrown rhododendron bushes are on fire,
every single one of them,
blazing like individual suns, the smell so different than
Elsie Davis preferred,
and she starts laughing a laugh she has never heard before or again.

Katie Jean Shinkle's THE ARSON PEOPLE is a winner of the **CCM•MAINLINE** Competition

For more info, point your browser to:

http://copingmechanisms.net/mainline/

OFFICIAL

CCM ◗

GET OUT OF JAIL
* VOUCHER *

- -

Tear this out.

Skip that social event.

It's okay.

You don't have to go if you don't want to. Pick up
the book you just bought. Open to the first page.
You'll thank us by the third paragraph.

If friends ask why you were a no-show, show them
this voucher.

You'll be fine.

- -

We're coping.

◗

CPSIA information can be obtained at www.ICGtesting.com
Printed in the USA
BVOW02s0304300415

398333BV00002B/11/P